Zia's Story

Shahnaz Qayumi

Zia's Story

illustrated by
Nahid Kazemi

TRADEWIND BOOKS
Vancouver • London

To my son Taras, who had to change his name.
He tasted adversity at a very young age, but the light in
his heart helped him persevere with life's journey—SQ

To the suffering Afghan people and
to all my Afghan friends—NK

CHAPTER ONE

The Kite Fight

The ticking clock next to my bed echoed in my head all night. I didn't sleep a wink, because my friends Hussain, Rustam, Timur and I were going to have a kite fight with some boys we didn't know—boys who were great kite-runners. Every boy in Kabul said they used something special to make their kite strings strong. Some said they mixed glue and crushed glass to strengthen them. That's why no one, not even a boy with perfect kite-flying skills, was able to cut the strings of their kites. Everyone dreamed of finding out their secret.

As I rushed out, *Moder* shouted from the kitchen, "Zia, don't be late for dinner!"

After school those boys met us outside the school playground, and we followed them to their neighbourhood.

We launched our kites into a sky already filled with kites, waving birds trapped in the wind. Our kites seemed to have minds of their own. We were about to lose hope when Rustam managed to cut the string of one of the other boys' kites. It flew off, celebrating its freedom like a bird of paradise. We started running after that kite sailing away in the sky, not paying attention to where we were going, because whoever finds a fallen kite gets to keep it.

Timur finally caught up to it, and we shouted, "Bravo, Timur!"

Behind us we heard the pounding footsteps and angry voices of the boys who had lost their kite during the game.

"We need to hide!" yelled Hussain.

Down an alley, I saw an open gate. "Let's hide over there!"

We were all out of breath.

"I hope they didn't see us come in here," Hussain said.

"What if it's one of their gardens," Rustam said.

"If it is, we're doomed," Timur said.

Just then a voice from behind us boomed, "Who are you boys, and what are you doing in my garden?"

We all froze.

An old man with a white beard, dressed in a white *shalwar kameez*, stood there. We were speechless.

"*Salam, Kaka Jan* . . . hello, Uncle," Hussain said.

"*Salam*," we all said.

"*Walaikum Assalam*, hello," the old man replied.

"We're sorry," I said. "We came into your garden without knocking,"

"So you just go into someone's garden?"

"Sorry, *Kaka Jan*," Timur said. "Some boys were chasing us. We were kite running, and we caught their loose kite."

"I haven't seen you in our neighbourhood before."

"We are from *Dea Sabz*," I said just as we heard the boys' voices from down the alley.

"That's Ajee Sahib's home," one of them said.

"Are you sure they went in there?" asked another.

"They must have."

Afraid, we looked at each other.

The old man whispered, pointing, "Hide behind those bushes and stay quiet."

Then he shouted down the alley, "What is going on? Why are you so loud out there?"

The boys came up to the garden gate. "Salam, Ajee Sahib. We saw four boys enter your garden."

Ajee Sahib asked, "So?"

"Those boys stole our kite."

"How? They took it from your home?" asked the old man.

None of the boys said a word.

"So why are you quiet now? Did you lose the kite fight?"

Silence.

"You know the rule. Whoever captures the kite, owns the kite. I want you all to go home. It is getting late, and your parents are waiting for you."

We were shocked.

"Go sit in the gazebo," he told us when the boys left. "You must be thirsty."

The gazebo floor was covered with red carpets. We sat on some cushions, and the old man came back carrying a tray set with glasses, a jug filled with *duogh*—a mix of yogurt, cucumber and mint—and a bowl full of brambleberries.

We all stood up.

"Please sit, all of you," he said. "Drink up!"

The cold duogh tasted good.

"I will take you home," the old man said after we

devoured the sweet juicy berries.

The sun was setting behind the mountains, and I realized that Moder would be upset I was late for dinner.

Ajee Sahib put a shawl on over his shoulders and said, "Boys, let's go before it gets too dark."

We didn't say a word until we got back to our neighbourhood.

"Show me where you live."

When we reached our alley, I pointed across the street. "That's where Hussain, Rustam and Timur live."

The old man walked over to my house and knocked on the door.

Pader's voice came from the other side of the door. "Who is there? Is it you, Zia?"

Ajee Sahib said, "Yes, brother. It is Zia. I brought him home."

"Salam, Ajee Sahib," Pader said, opening the door. "Is everything all right?"

"Oh yes, everything is fine. I'll take the other boys home too. Goodnight."

"Many thanks. God bless you. It is dinner time. I would be delighted if you joined us."

"No, thank you. My family will expect me for dinner."

Inside, I told Pader and Moder what happened. "Ajee helped us, even though we were strangers."

"If someone takes refuge with you, you must protect them, feed them and take care of them," Moder said. "That's the Afghan code of honour, you know— *Nanawatai*."

"You have to give sanctuary to someone who asks for help."

After dinner I played chess with Pader. Then I went to bed happy because tomorrow was Friday, *jumah*, our day of prayer, when we would go to my grandparents for lunch or visit my uncles and aunts, or my father's friends would drop by to chat and drink tea. I thought about what happened that day—the kite fight, the chase, the old man in the garden and what my parents said about the Afghan custom of providing refuge.

Suddenly there was a loud and persistent knocking on the front door. "Open the door!" From the stairway landing, I watched Pader open the door halfway to see who was there. Moder stood behind him.

The door flew open. Three soldiers holding guns and two men dressed in suits pushed their way inside.

"Salam, *Khairat ast*. Good evening. Is everything all

right?" Pader asked.

"We need you to come with us."

"Why? Did I do something wrong?"

"We can't talk here. You must come with us."

Moder froze, then broke down crying.

The soldiers took Pader's arms and tried to pull him outside, but he stood his ground. "Can I have a word with my son."

"Just for a minute," one of them said. "We don't have time to wait."

I walked down the stairs and hugged him tightly. Pader looked deep into my eyes and whispered, "You are now the man of our family, Zia. Until I return home. Take care of your mother."

I never shared that moment with anyone, not even with Moder. It is a secret between Pader and me.

CHAPTER TWO

I Am a Man

We never heard from Pader again. He vanished from our lives, but I never gave up hope that one day he'd walk through our front door and give us a hug.

Moder kept watch over me. I had to stay close to home because the streets were patrolled by armed police and soldiers knocking on doors and dragging away our neighbours.

Each night after I finished my homework, I took a candle into my room and read *One Thousand and One Nights* before going to sleep. One night while I was reading, a massive explosion shook the room. The windows to the front room were blown out, and the houses across the street collapsed.

I shouted, "Moder, are you okay?"

She came into my bedroom, pulled me close and held me so tight I could hardly breathe.

"What happened?" I asked.

"It's nothing," she said, kissing me on the forehead.

"Go back to sleep. It's only construction."

"In the middle of the night?"

"Sometimes there is an emergency, and it doesn't matter what time it is."

I closed my eyes till the morning light woke me. Moder was sitting at the kitchen table wearing the same clothes as the day before.

"Moder . . ."

Her eyes were red and she looked worried.

"If you want to, you can sleep later today."

"No, I'll be late for school."

She put her hand on my head. "You'll stay home from school today."

The front room was a mess, with shattered glass everywhere. Across the street, the houses were flattened—a smoking pile of rubble. *Hussain, Rustam, Timur!* I felt Moder's hand on my shoulder and looked up at her face.

She looked shaken. "Don't worry about your friends. I'm sure they got away."

"What about school?" Our school was behind Rustam's

house. "Where will I go to study?"

Moder sighed. "Go to your room and change. Then we'll have breakfast and talk."

I turned on the TV.

"Zia, there is no electricity."

For a long time, we had no electricity. We burned candles to light the house. Moder cooked our food outside on a wood fire. I collected fallen tree branches and wood to feed the fire.

From then on, Moder always covered her hair with a *chador* when she went out. And she stopped teaching at the university. "The university and every girls' school is closed," she told me one day. "Women are not allowed to go outside alone anymore."

"Why?"

"The Taliban. They don't allow women to work or girls to go to school."

Soon there was no more public music or dancing. Instead, there was a curfew. Police stood at every corner. Men had to grow their beards. Women had to cover themselves from head to toe.

* * *

One day Moder said, "Zia, we are running out of money. You need to start working."

"I will take care of you," I said.

She opened up her arms and hugged me. "I am so glad to have a son like you. I will cook *bowlanie* every day, and you can sell it in the market."

So every morning the house filled with the smell of those flatbreads filled with chives or potatoes.

And every morning Moder would ask me to taste one. "How is it, Zia? Is there enough salt and pepper?"

"Delicious!" I would say. It was true.

She would put a heavy tray of bowlanie on my head, and out the door I would go. I had to walk straight or the tray would tilt and all the bowlanie would fall to the ground.

I couldn't go to the market square, because other boys were there selling food, so I would walk up and down streets shouting, "Hot and crispy bowlanie, homemade, only ten afghanis! Hurry, before it's all gone!"

Most days I would sell all of them.

Moder also started an underground home school. If the Taliban government found out, she would be punished.

One day Moder said, "*Zia, Khala* Zahra doesn't have a son. You need to go with her to the judge, because her husband's cousins are trying to take her house."

So I became our neighbourhood "man" for all the widows with no sons. Some days after selling our bowlanie, I would go with one of the neighbourhood widows to the market. All the women called me *bacha jaan*, dear son. They would give me tea with some dried fruits. I understood finally what Pader meant when he whispered in my ear, "You are now a man. Take care of your mother." But he didn't think that I would become a man not only for Moder but also for all the neighbourhood widows.

I sorely missed my friends Hussain, Rustam and Timur.

CHAPTER THREE

The Burned House Mystery

Dark nights without light, cold rooms without heat, and endless gunshots. Blood on the street didn't shock us anymore. People only thought about how to save their own families.

One day Moder sat me down when I got back from selling on the street. "We have to leave Kabul."

My friends had disappeared without a trace. There were no celebrations anymore—no weddings, no holidays. We couldn't listen to music. What was left of our neighbourhood was slowly disappearing. Moder's home school was thinning out—fewer and fewer students showed up. People were afraid.

I was very lonely. Moder's eyes were always red. Sometimes we even had to burn our books and our chairs to keep warm.

"This is not living. It's barely surviving," she said.

"We must leave."

One day Moder said, "We are going to visit Bobo Gul."
  "Why?"
  "I need to see her. We'll take the bus."

We got off the bus and walked a long way until we reached a house that was half-burned. It had a big hole in the garden. Two young girls were playing there. "This is Bobo Gul's house. Zia, go and knock on the door. I'll wait here."
  I knocked two times very gently at the door and waited, but no one answered.
  "Knock harder!"
  Finally, Bobo Gul opened the door.
  "Salam, Bobo Gul Jaan," Moder said as she drew closer.
  They started kissing each other's faces and holding each other's hands. Bobo Gul opened the door wide. "Welcome, please come inside the house."
  An old man was sitting down on the sofa.
  "Shah Agh, this is my son, Zia," Moder said.
  Shah Agh kissed me on the cheek. "I am so happy to see you, Zia. Look at you! You are all grown up now

and taking care of your moder. Your father is a wonderful man. He will come home soon."

"Bobo Gul, what happened to your beautiful rose garden?" Moder asked.

"Bombs. Thanks be to Allah that my family is alive."

Moder turned to me and said abruptly, "Zia, go outside and play with Bobo Gul's grandchildren."

I have no idea what they talked about inside that half-burned house. After a while Bobo Gul and Shah Agh came outside with Moder and wished us well.

When we got back home, Moder went straight to her closet and brought out a few shoe boxes, one on top of the other. "We need more money." She took out her beautiful handbags with matching shoes from the boxes. "Tomorrow, take these into town and sell them."

CHAPTER FOUR

Goodbye Sweet Home

One day Moder said, "Zia, go to the market and buy four *naan*."

I loved the market with flowers and fruit piled high. I liked watching the people bargain.

I bought four naan and rushed back home. On my way there, a flock of blackbirds flew in formation over the dry and dusty grass. In the distance, a whistle blew.

By the time I got home, a huge full moon was rising in the darkening sky.

I made a wish: "Please. Please, let Pader come home to us."

The wind blew harder, and birds cried out above me. I looked around. Dark ruins, dark houses with no lights, a deserted street. Moder was asleep on the couch when I stepped in, so I put the naan on the kitchen table and went to my room. But my bed was gone. I went to Moder's room. Her bed was gone as well.

I rushed over to my sleeping mother. "Moder!" I said, waking her up. "What happened to our beds?"

"I sold them to make some money for our trip. We are leaving tonight."

I was stunned.

I couldn't imagine living anywhere else. I had lived in that house, on that street, in that neighbourhood, my entire life. I was scared to leave and angry at Moder for keeping such a secret.

"Where are we going? What about Pader?" I asked. "Why do we have to leave?"

"I asked Shah Agh to help me find someone to get us out. He found someone. We have to leave tonight. We will go with another family so we won't be alone. I will answer all your questions once we are on the road."

I had a thousand questions. *What if Pader comes back and we are not here?*

Moder put her hand under my chin and held it. "I am so sorry that this feels so sudden, and I didn't tell you until now. I didn't want to worry you." She put her arms around me and hugged me tightly.

"We can't take very much with us. One small suitcase."

"But how will we travel?"

"First by minibus, then pickup truck."

"Who will live in our house?" I asked.

"I don't know, bacha jaan. We can't sell our house. The Taliban will stop us if they think we are fleeing."

"What if Pader comes back and we are not here?"

"Once we are in Pakistan, I will call your uncle and give him our contact information. Change into those clothes," she said, pointing to the shalwar kameez I only wore on special days.

I went to my room and stared at all my belongings— my footballs, my books and my kites. I picked up everything one by one, touching them and holding them and saying goodbye to each one. I would miss everything.

I changed into my traditional clothes. At the doorway, I stopped and looked back at the room that held so many memories.

"I have to leave you behind," I whispered. I looked at my things. "I don't have room in our suitcase. You will be safer here." I closed the door. *I hope no one will come here until I get back.*

In her bedroom, Moder was holding her diploma. "I can't take this with me," she said. "If soldiers search us, they'll know we are running away. We have to say we are travelling to our cousin's wedding in Logar province. I'll wear a burqa."

She smiled at me. "You look very handsome in those clothes."

Just then there was a knock at the door. "If it is the neighbours, don't say anything about leaving."

The knocking grew louder.

"Do you want me to answer it?" I asked.

"No, I will do it," she finally said, opening the door. "Salam, dear brother."

A man was there. "We've come to give you and your son a ride. The other family is already in the minibus. Please hurry."

"Many thanks. We will be out shortly."

She turned to me. "Zia, it's time to leave."

The man grabbed the suitcase. "I will take it to the car for you. Hurry."

"God bless you, brother," Moder said. "Come, Zia!"

I followed her out.

I couldn't look at her, because my face was covered in tears. "I left a light on so people will think we are at home."

Then she locked the door.

I whispered goodbye to our home as I stepped into the minibus.

CHAPTER FIVE

Burqa, Safe Haven

Moder said "Salam" to the strangers as we took the seats behind the driver. I did the same. There were two women wearing blue burqas and an old man sitting beside them. A young man sat all alone at the very back.

Soon we saw Kabul—our city—roll by, and we were transferred to the bed of a pickup truck. We rode through the desert on unpaved roads to avoid checkpoints. The road was bumpy and we were bounced hard, up and down. Moder pulled a couple of sweaters out of our suitcase and folded them for me to sit on. She put her arms around me, and I felt safer sitting close to her.

We passed through tall rocky mountains. Every time my eyes closed, the truck would bounce hard and I would wake up.

After more than two hours, the driver stopped in front of a small house. "We will stay here tonight," he said.

Inside, lots of people were sitting on a carpet. A boy came by with a basin of water and a cloth for us to wash and dry our hands. He spread a tablecloth on the floor in front of us. Another boy came over with fresh flatbread and a bowl of soup with potatoes and carrots.

We all slept in that same room. Men slept on one side, and women and children slept on the other. It was hard to sleep with all the snoring.

Mother woke me early in the morning. "Zia, wake up, dear son. We need to get ready."

"It's still dark," I said.

"We will leave soon, before the other people wake up."

The sun was rising from behind the mountains, and birds were singing.

We washed quickly in the creek. The water was so clear that I could see the rocks and the green creek bed. I went back to where my group sat around a white cloth beneath a tree.

"Zia, come sit beside me." Moder made room for me next to her.

We ate, and then we all climbed back into the pickup truck. It started with a loud noise and dust flew on our faces.

After a few more hours of bumpy roads, the truck

stopped and a resounding voice ordered us out.

A man holding a rifle asked, "Where are you going?"

"We are going to Logar province for a wedding," the driver said.

"Hey, you, come down here," someone else barked at the young man travelling with us. "You need to fight for your country."

The young man looked terrified. One of the women said, "Please don't take him away from me. He is the only child I have, and I am a widow."

"I am also the only son of a widow," the first man said, turning to the young man. "Come with us and make your country proud of you."

"Please let him escort me!" the woman pleaded, but two more armed men jumped up onto the truck and dragged the young man off.

"Please, in the name of God, leave my son alone. If you are taking him, then also take me. I have no one but him. He is my life."

My mother spoke up. "Dear brother. Please have one thousand afghanis for the struggle." She handed the money to the old man to pass over to them, and they released the young passenger.

We were all terrified as we drove away. The young

man said to my mother and to the lady who pretended to be his mother, "Many thanks, aunties. God bless you both. You saved my life. I don't know how to thank you."

"Thanks be to God," Moder said. And then she said to me, "Don't be afraid, son. Everything will be over soon."

CHAPTER SIX

Safe at Last

"Zia, wake up. We are out of Afghanistan. We are safe."

We had arrived at the market in Quetta, across the border in Pakistan, and we bought spicy takeout food—so hot I could hardly eat it. We found a rundown motel, and the first thing I did was take a shower. Moder looked at her burqa and our filthy clothes and said, "I don't think it is even worth washing these. We will throw them away."

"But I want to keep my jacket," I said.

"Okay. I'll wash it."

The next day, Moder and I started looking for a place to stay.

Moder had brought enough money to pay for four months' rent in advance, and we shared a room with another Afghan family. That was nearly all the money we had. But there was enough for a celebration meal. Moder and I picked up a huge tray filled with *palaw*, eggplant with dried yogurt, and *kofta* from an Afghan restaurant close by our motel.

Moder invited a neighbour, Khadija, with her little daughter. Khadija brought a blanket and pillows for us.

"I am Aisha," Moder said. "And this is my only child, Zia. My husband was taken from our home when President Najibullah was in power, and he never came back. We don't know if he is alive or dead. I went many times to Pulicharkhie jail to look for him, but the big *Khad* told me not to bother going there anymore. I pray every day that he is alive."

The next day, we started looking for jobs. We knocked on every single door in the neighbourhood to ask if they needed help with cleaning their houses or washing their clothes. No one needed any help, even though they could see that we were refugees with no money. We sat under a tree and ate the leftover ground beef curry wrapped in naan for lunch.

"Let's go to the market and look there for a job," Moder said after we ate.

* * *

In the market, young boys worked in grocery stores, shoe stores, bakeries, tea rooms and restaurants. I told Moder I could do that kind of job.

"If I cannot find anything, then maybe you will work, but I would like you to study and go to school."

An old man stopped in front of Mother and placed ten rupees in her hand. "God bless you," she said to the old man, "but my son and I are looking for a job. If your wife needs any help at home cooking, washing or cleaning, I would be happy to help."

The old man wrote something on a piece of paper and handed it to her. "Here is my address. Come to my home tomorrow morning."

"*Manana*. Many thanks. We will come tomorrow." And turning to me, she said, "I will find out from Khadija where the school for refugee children is and enroll you tomorrow."

We left early in the morning to find the house. After Moder knocked on the old man's door, a young man opened it.

"We were asked to come and help Ajee Sahib's wife."

"Yes, Ajee Sahib told us you would come. Please come inside."

"Thank you, but I'd like to see his wife," Moder said.

"She is not home," the young man told us.

"Okay, we will come back when she is home."

"Ajee Sahib is waiting for you inside."

"Zia, let's leave," Moder said to me.

"We will pay a lot and you won't even have to work."

Moder pulled me away. "Let's run, Zia. These are bad people!"

We were both out of breath when we got home. Khadija must have heard us come in, because she opened the window and asked if everything was all right. Moder started to cry and Khadija came over.

"Tell me what happened," she said.

Mother told her everything. "Horrible man," she said. "God will punish him."

I was devastated and wanted to take revenge. The next night, when Moder was busy in the kitchen with Khadija, I slipped out quietly and went to the old man's house. I threw rocks over the wall and broke their window then took off and ran home as fast as I could.

Moder was waiting for me behind the door with tears in her eyes. As soon as she saw me, she was relieved.

"Zia, you scared me. Where did you go?" she asked, hugging me.

"I went to the old man's house and broke his window with rocks."

"Zia, I appreciate that you tried to protect me, but I don't believe in taking revenge. Revenge is a code of honour in our culture that I don't want you to follow. Revenge only brings hatred, and in the end no one wins."

"I'm so sorry, I'll never do that again."

Soon, Khadija introduced Moder to a woman named Fahim and her family, and she started working for them. Moder and I would leave early in the morning and come back home after she washed their dinner dishes.

I didn't go to the refugee school after all, because it was very far from where we lived. When Moder got her first paycheck, she bought me books and notebooks.

I helped her water Fahim's gardens and take care of their flowers. Moder would give me homework to do while she cooked and cleaned. I sat under a big tree in their yard and did my homework. In the evening, she marked my work and taught me new things.

I was very lonely. I dreamed of being back home like in the old days, playing with my friends and sleeping in my own room.

Fahim's family was nice and treated my mother with respect. I think they heard from Khadija that she had been a teacher back in Kabul. Mother listened to the news on an old radio Khadija had given us. She read the newspapers after Khadija's husband had finished reading them.

"Afghanistan is going back to the dark ages," Moder told me one night. "I have lost hope."

We heard from Khadija that a passport would cost us three thousand dollars. We decided to save enough money to buy false passports to escape.

CHAPTER SEVEN

Our Savings

The situation back home went from bad to worse. Khadija's family finally got papers to settle in America, and the landlord started showing the apartment to new tenants. The end of the month came quickly, and Khadija's family left Pakistan. Mother and I felt very lonely once again. The rooms were rented to four young single men, and Moder lost her privacy. She had to keep her chador tied even in the kitchen when cooking. She asked me to help her in the kitchen so she wouldn't be alone with the strange men.

Almost every night, the men had friends over and sat talking and laughing late into the evening. A few times when we came back from Fahim's in the evening, we found the door wide open. We kept the door to our room locked.

One such night when we returned from Fahim's house, the door to our room was wide open.

"Moder, our door is open!"

"Zia, let me go in first."

We stepped inside the room together, turned on the lights and saw that our room had been turned upside down. The money that Moder had been saving was gone. She sat on the floor and sobbed.

I tidied the room. In the other room, the men were laughing and chatting.

CHAPTER EIGHT

Shattered Hopes

When I woke up the next day, my mother was still asleep. She was usually up before me, so I wondered what was going on.

"I am awake." She looked pale, and her eyes were swollen and red. "Can you please go to Fahim's and tell them that I am not feeling well today."

I hesitated.

"Don't worry. I will be all right. On your way, buy a lock so we can fix our door."

Before going to Fahim's family, I knocked on the door of the four men. There was no sound from inside, so I knocked on the door harder and harder.

A man opened the door. He looked half-asleep. "What do you need, kid?"

"Someone broke into our room yesterday."

"So what?"

"You guys leave the apartment door open all the time."

The man rubbed his eyes and said, "Why didn't you tell us last night? We leave the door open so you can get in."

"But we have a key. My mother works for a family till eight at night. Our savings were stolen."

His face dropped. "I will tell everyone to lock the outside door from now on."

I felt a bit better, having confronted him, even though he didn't apologize.

Moder's condition got worse. She couldn't even stand. She lost her job at Fahim's. I started to look for a job in the market. I finally got a job at a kebabie fast food and takeout restaurant. The owner had just a few tables and needed a boy to fan the coal while the meat was cooking.

I started work that same day with a handmade fan. I also had to wash the skewers at the end of the day. Ustad, the boss, showed me how to soak them in water. I worked with another boy, a bit older than me, called Najib. He served the customers and was in charge of making tea.

My hands got tired from shaking the fan, especially during lunch and dinner, when we had lots of customers. I had to vigorously shake it to keep the ash off the coal. Najib and I were always busy cleaning and sweeping. We ate together or drank green tea with cardamom, sweetened with sugar. I was happy to have a job.

Moder grew quieter and quieter. She no longer asked me how my day was. She slept most of the day and didn't do any chores or cooking. I brought her food and tried to feed her. She would always refuse to eat, saying that she had eaten already. I had to do all the cleaning and washing and didn't have time to study. Moder grew thinner every day. I decided to take her to a doctor as soon as I got my paycheck.

Because Moder was so weak, we took a taxi. After a thorough examination, the doctor said that Moder was physically healthy but very depressed. I wondered how your mind could be so ill while your body is healthy.

The doctor asked, "Has anything bad happened to her recently?"

"All our money was stolen," I said. "Since then, she has slept most of the time. The curtains are down during the day, and she doesn't want to do anything.

She is getting weaker and weaker."

He listened to me carefully and said, "Son, what you are describing are the signs of a depressed person. If a person's mind is not healthy, their physical health can be destroyed."

"Can you help her get better?"

"Let me explain . . ." he began just as we heard a knock on the office door. "I am not finished with this patient. Please don't bother us," he called out loudly, then continued. "Son, what is your name?"

"Zia."

"You see, dear Zia, I hope you understand what I am trying to say, because you are very young." He came closer. "Those savings were a window to freedom for you both. Now her hope of escaping is shattered."

I saw sense in what he said.

"I treat lots of Afghans with similar symptoms—when a person loses hope, their physical health suffers. I will prescribe some medication for your mother. You must give her hope by having courage yourself."

On the way home, I bought Moder's medication.

I got to work a bit late that day. Ustad was not happy with me. I had missed the busy lunch rush. I apologized and told him that I had to take Moder to the doctor.

I was exhausted, and my hands had no strength to keep fanning the fire. Finally, a little after three o'clock, we took a break. I felt extra tired. It had been a long day.

CHAPTER NINE

Losing Another Friend

Najib and I grew closer every day. One day during our lunch break, he said, "Zia, I am going to start studying soon." I was so happy for him—that he had decided to go to school rather than work at the restaurant.

"What great news! So, you don't have to support your family anymore?"

He shook his head and said, "I must support my mother and three sisters. My father is dead, and I don't have a brother. I am the breadwinner. I don't know if you remember a big group of boys that was here for lunch last week. They were very friendly. They asked me if I would like to go to school. I told them it is my dream to get an education and that I went to school back home in Afghanistan, but here I have to support my family. They were so kind and told me that they could help me study for free. They said the school would support my mother and my sisters too."

"Wow. You are a lucky boy."

"Yes, that is exactly what I am going to do. I already told Ustad I am leaving."

Very soon after that, Najib left his job. It was tough to lose another friend, and work doubled because I was doing both jobs until Ustad could find a replacement for Najib.

It was the end of the month, the time when Ustad paid me. When he gave me my salary, it was way more than what I had been getting before. "Zia, what do you think about getting a raise in salary, and I won't bother hiring a new person?"

Although it would be a lot more work, I was happy that I could make some extra money, so I agreed.

I knew what I was going to do with the extra money—I went straight to the bookstore in the market. I asked for one of Rumi's poetry books for my mother. I knew how much she enjoyed Rumi's poetry. Sometimes she would call me out of bed, saying, "Zia, listen to this poem." From then on, I read her one of Rumi's poems every night and would ask her to explain the meaning to me.

A month went by fast because I was busy at the restaurant all day. On payday I went into a candy shop on my way home and bought some *sheer pira*, Afghan rosewater and cardamom fudge, for Moder. They were a favourite treat of hers.

When I got home, I gave her a wrapped sheer pira. She smiled and thanked me. I gave her my earnings and said, "We are going to save this for our trip."

CHAPTER TEN

The Miracle of Madrassa

Months later, Najib came to visit me one day as I was finishing work. We hugged. He was dressed in a clean shalwar kameez and wore a small white hat.

"Zia, I have good news for you," he said. "I told my teachers about you and how much you love to go to school. They agreed to take you."

Right away I thought about how happy this news would make Moder. "Najib, that's the best news I could ever dream of. But I need my earnings to pay for our rent and food."

"They will pay for that too!" he said. "I will bring you there tomorrow and you can speak to the imam yourself."

The next day after work, I went with Najib to the school and spoke to his teacher. Yes! It was true. There were no fees to pay and I would get money for our rent and groceries. My mind was full of dreams of the future. I was so eager to get home and give the news to my mother.

As soon as I arrived home, I told her about the school.

"I am glad to hear that," she said. "But can you wait until the beginning of the school year? I will get more energy and start working, and then you can go to school."

"It's a refugee school for Afghan boys, and it offers free schooling."

A real smile spread on my mother's lips. She raised her arms and I hugged her. It felt like the old days. "I'll start working again and will be able to buy you books, notebooks, pens and pencils."

"They will provide everything, Moder!" I told her excitedly. "They will pay for our rent and groceries too!"

After a couple of weeks, Ustad found a much older busboy to replace me. I thanked him, got my last paycheck and was very much looking forward to my new life.

The next morning, I got up early and prepared breakfast for Moder before leaving home. The school was a long way from where we lived, but I knew the city very well by then and got there easily. The principal of the school greeted me. He asked me to step into his office to give me my books and some information about the school. He showed me a list of rules hanging on the wall: students were forbidden from reading newspapers, playing games or doing any personal activities inside the *madrassa*, and casual chatter, joking or fooling about of any kind would not be tolerated. In the classroom, students were to read only the Koran.

As soon as the clock struck eleven, boys spilled out of the classroom into the yard for a break. "That is your class," the principal said, pointing. "The teacher already knows you will be joining today."

I thanked the principal and walked out of his office toward the classroom. There was no noise and no jostling. Instead, the boys walked in an orderly manner, heads bowed respectfully and eyes downcast to avoid my stare. The boys were dressed in ankle-length white shalwar kameez and white skullcaps. Their feet were bare.

I found the school very different than the school I had attended in Afghanistan.

Najib was in the older boys' class, but we usually had lunch together—if he was not busy in the principal's office. He was not the same Najib I once knew. We used to joke and laugh a lot during our short break time. He had been very relaxed and, like a stand-up comedian, would mimic Ustad's walking and how he would order us around. At school, he was different. He didn't joke anymore and was much quieter.

One lunch hour during my third week of school, I saw someone very familiar to me. I quickly walked closer to see if I was right and couldn't believe my eyes.

It was one of my best friends from Kabul. Timur! He wasn't looking at me. He was busy talking to a boy sitting next to him. I stood there for a few seconds, but he still hadn't seen me. I was too impatient to talk to him, so I called his name. "Timur!"

He quickly turned his face toward me, and as he laid eyes on me, his mouth dropped wide open.

"Zia! Is it you?" He jumped toward me, and we hugged each other tightly for a few seconds before realizing that everyone was staring at us. This behaviour was not allowed at school. We separated and became quiet. I had tears in my eyes but tried not to show them.

We were both looking at each other from head to toe for a few minutes. Timur looked pale and way older than his real age.

I had many questions for him, so I raised my voice and said, "Timur, I can't believe I'm seeing you so far away from home. I am happy to see you alive. Moder was right to say you would be all right. Tell me what happened after the bombings that terrible night."

"I was at my cousin's house that night, which is why I survived, but my whole family—my mother, father and little sister—was killed that night. I didn't find out until three days later. My uncle told me what happened. He suggested that I don't go home, so I can keep my good memories alive. He held a funeral for my family. I couldn't believe that I'd become an orphan overnight. I wished that I had died with them, so I didn't have to go on living thinking about them."

"I'm so sorry," I said. I thought about his little sister and choked back a sob.

"I still wanted to see our home with my own eyes. One day I snuck out and went back to our neighbourhood to see for myself. As soon as I turned onto our street, I saw from afar that there was nothing left but ruins. I was so upset that I didn't even look at the other side of the street where your home was. I decided never to go back to the neighbourhood where I was born and where I had all my memories."

Timur gestured to the boy sitting next to him. "I apologize for not introducing my cousin. This is Safie."

I said hello to Safie and shook his hand. I was shattered to hear Timur's story.

"How did you end up coming here to Pakistan and this madrassa?" I asked Timur.

"My uncle lost his business in Kabul, and the situation was getting worse, so he decided to take us to Pakistan. I know he was upset about everything and feeling useless because he had a big family plus me to take care of and could hardly feed us. He had no job, no money. He had a heart attack and died soon after we came here."

"I am sorry to hear about your uncle. Life has became so hard for us Afghans."

The school bell interrupted our conversation. We got up.

"Zia, let's meet here after class," Timur said.

It was a miracle to find my lost friend far away from home in the madrassa.

After school I rushed to where Timur and I had met earlier.

"Tell me about how Aunt Aisha is doing," he said.

"I must hurry home to her now, but tomorrow I'll tell you my story. And I will take you home to see Moder. You will cheer her up. She will be so happy to see you."

"Tomorrow morning I am going on a mission for the madrassa."

We said goodbye to each other. I left school feeling happy to have finally found one of my best friends and hoped to see Hussain and Rustam one day.

When I got home, I told Moder about Timur. "He is alive and goes to my school."

"That's wonderful!"

"But his family was killed in the explosion," I said, avoiding her eyes. Moder pulled me close.

I couldn't wait for Timur to be back from his mission the next day. I got up early. Moder was already up, with the breakfast bread and tea ready for me for the first time in a long while. I was so happy to see my life getting back to something like normal. My mother was feeling better and my friend was alive.

I arrived a bit early to the madrassa because I was eager to talk to Timur, but after several minutes of waiting, I felt anxious. It was still early so I decided to go to his class to look for him. The boys in the madrassa sat in long rows, so I could see all of them in the classroom, but Timur wasn't there. I waited until lunch break and quickly went to see Safie to find out if Timur was back from the mission. Safie said no, but that maybe he would be back tomorrow.

A week passed and I didn't see or hear from Timur. He didn't come to school. I kept asking his cousin if Timur was back, and every time he said, "We are all waiting for him at home but have not heard from him."

A month passed. I told Safie one day that maybe we should go and see the principal and ask him, because it was the madrassa's mission. Safie said he had already been to the principal's office a couple of times, but he didn't know anything. As soon as he heard of Timur, the principal said, he would come personally to tell us and we should wait to hear from him.

From then on, I spent my breaks with Najib and Safie. I was getting used to the madrassa. As long as we obeyed the rules, recited the verses of the Koran—even if we didn't know the meaning—we were okay. At this level, our teacher would read a few verses from the Koran and ask a student to repeat it. When he was satisfied, he sent us off to commit the verses to memory. We returned when we could demonstrate to him that we had learned the lesson, and he would teach us new verses.

Three months passed and Timur didn't come back. I regretted not spending more time on telling him my story that day, but I had to rush home after school to give Moder her medication, as I did every day—something I couldn't neglect. I was very hopeful I might see him again one day.

Soon after, our neighbours knocked to say there was a long-distance call from Canada. It was Khadija.

"Khadija kept her promise to call us," Moder said. She asked me to talk, passing the receiver to me.

I said hello to Auntie Khadija.

"I have good news for you, Zia," she said. "The Canadian government is accepting refugees from Afghanistan. You and your moder must go to the Canadian Embassy in Islamabad as soon as you can."

She gave me her phone number and asked me to call when we had news.

I thanked our neighbours for letting us use their phone.

CHAPTER ELEVEN

Enlightenments and Suspicions

Moder seemed happy and was thankful for Khadija. Although it was good news, I was still thinking about Timur.

My mother noticed that I was not as excited about the news as she was.

"Zia, you'll miss your school, won't you?"

"We don't learn anything but the Koran at school anyway. And it is in Arabic, so I don't even understand it. All we do is memorize verses."

My mother's face dropped. "You are not in a regular school?"

"No. I am going to a madrassa."

Mother's face turned white, like she'd seen a ghost. She showed me an article in the newspaper. According to the article, madrassas in Pakistan were training future members of the Taliban. In some cases, students were being trained to carry out suicide bombings.

"We'll leave tonight on the overnight bus to Islamabad. The bus will take fourteen to fifteen hours. We will arrive early in the morning and go straight to the Canadian Embassy. I already packed our savings," she said. "That way we can be at the embassy before they open."

"I'll go to the madrassa and say goodbye to Najib."

"Don't tell him you are leaving for Canada."

It was early morning prayers when I arrived at the madrassa. The gate was wide open.

When I saw Najib, his head was down and he was walking fast to get to class on time. "Hey, Najib!" I called. I pulled the newspaper from my pocket, opened it to the article and held it right to his face. He glanced at it, then, with anger in his voice, said, "You believe these lies! Do you believe the Afghan government? They are all corrupt. You know that. I don't want to see you. Get lost."

"Najib, please listen to me."

He spun around and walked away without turning back to look at me, probably for the last time. I was heartbroken. I didn't know how to open his eyes. I thought he was my friend.

Then I saw Safie. Holding the newspaper to his face, I told him to leave the madrassa.

He grabbed the newspaper. "Oh no! Is it true?" He seemed to believe me. "Why did your family send you and Timur to the madrassa?" I asked.

"Family friends told us about the madrassa. Pader didn't know the truth about it. I don't know what to do."

"You have to leave."

I ripped up the article, stuffed it in my pocket and went to the kebab restaurant where I had worked with Najib to say goodbye to Ustad.

The market was crowded and noisy. I saw Ustad from afar, standing over a table of guests and talking to them. His eyes landed on me. "Zia, is it you? Come closer. I thought you forgot about me."

I was delighted to see him and walked quickly toward him. He had his arms wide open, and we hugged and shook hands. Turning back to his customers, he said, "I apologize for the impoliteness, but do you know who this is? Zia is one of my old, hard-working employees. He is like a son to me. I haven't seen him for so long. I will get back to you shortly."

He pulled a chair close to where he barbecued and

asked me to sit. "I will barbecue some meat for you."

I had no money with me, so I said, "Thank you, no, Ustad."

"You are my guest. I am happy to see you after so long. How is your school going? Is your mother feeling better?"

I told him about the madrassa.

"I knew it, because nobody gives you anything for free, not even for one day. When those boys took Najib, I was suspicious. I told him not to go there. It seemed too good to be true. I'm glad you got out of it."

As mother predicted, it was 5 a.m. when we arrived in Islamabad. We bought some fresh naan from a bakery and went to the Canadian Embassy, where we were the first people at the door. Within an hour, twenty or thirty Afghans were standing in the line behind us, and more were arriving, all hoping to make Canada their home. Many were women with young children.

We were received by the high commissioner with respect, especially when they heard that Moder was a single mother and a former university teacher. When they asked if she was married, she told them about my father's disappearance and not knowing if he was still alive or dead. They told us we would hear back from them in four to six months.

CHAPTER TWELVE

Light at the End
of the Tunnel

While we waited for our visas to Canada, Moder began teaching at an Afghan refugee school, and I started at a school too.

Six months later, we received a letter saying that our application was approved. The Canadian government loaned us money to buy plane tickets. We had no passports, so we were issued travel documents by the Red Cross. When we arrived in Ottawa, an immigration officer accompanied us to a hotel. In the taxi, all I could see were trees.

I woke up early the next day and saw an empty street with fancy shops along a tree-lined boulevard.

Moder called Khadija in Toronto and thanked her. We flew to Calgary that same day and soon found an apartment. Moder found work during the day as a seamstress and took evening English classes. I enrolled in a school, but since it was just before the summer holidays, I signed up for a summer English class.

My teacher introduced me to the class, saying, "Students! Please welcome Zia to his new home in Canada."

All the students shouted, "Welcome, Zia!"

"If he needs help, please help him in any way you can," the teacher said. "He is still learning English, therefore please speak to him slowly."

Moder started dressing like she used to, without a chador.

I worried all the time about Timur. Moder knew there was something bothering me.

"Zia, you seem worried. What is it?" When I didn't answer, she asked, "Is it about Timur?"

"Yes, when I saw him last, he said he was going on a mission."

Her eyes filled with tears. "Timur grew up in a family where there was respect. I don't think he would destroy other people's lives."

CHAPTER THIRTEEN

Zia's Story

It was the first day of school after a long and lonely summer. I was looking forward to the start of a new school year. Maybe I could make new friends like Timur, Rustam and Hussain.

In geography, we were given an assignment to write about our home country. It was painful to think about all I had left behind—about Pader, about our beautiful home where I had been so happy. The rest of the day passed in a blur, my head full of dark memories.

A few days later, when I came home, Moder was waiting for me. Just as my fingers reached for the doorbell, the door flew open. She had a big smile and held out her arms for me.

I whispered, "Salam, hello."

"How was your day, Zia?" Her voice shook me out of my gloomy thoughts.

"Can you help me with my geography assignment?"

"Of course, I would love to. Let's talk about it over a cup of tea."

I loved teatime. Moder had a pot of green tea with cardamom ready, and a plate full of dried fruit was waiting for us on the table.

"So what is the assignment?"

"We have to write about where we grew up. It's making me anxious to write about it."

"Why?"

"There's a lot I don't even remember."

"When you were young, Pader used to take you around the city. He would say, '*Buod Nabud, Yag bacha buod.*' He would show you the tall mountains, the white clouds, the burning sun, the fruits hanging from trees, the vegetable sellers in the market. Don't you remember? You can write about that."

Happy memories flooded back to me. I went to my bedroom, with Pader's voice ringing in my ears: *Buod Nabud, Yag bacha buod.*

I sat staring at the globe in my room, spinning it with my index finger. My finger rested on the land-locked country in Central Asia called Afghanistan, where I once lived.

I closed my eyes and saw myself running over deserts and snow-covered mountains under a blue sky. The grass was green, the trees full of fruit. The river ran cold from the mountains.

"Zia, are you finished with your homework? It is dinner time."

"No. I am only halfway through."

"Come and eat, then finish later."

Moder had invited friends for dinner, and they were laughing and chatting loudly. On the table was my favourite dish, *Qabuli* palaw, a rice dish with lamb. It reminded me of a time when I was at Hussain's house for lunch and we had the same meal.

I remembered Hussain's mother putting the last piece of meat on my plate, adding rice and saying, "Eat, my son. *Nosh e Jan*. Please enjoy it."

In Afghanistan, no matter how rich or poor you are, you always serve your guest first.

"Are you all right, Zia? You are so quiet."

"Yes, Moder. I am just thinking about my geography assignment. I am sorry for leaving the table, but I have to finish my assignment. It is due tomorrow."

Everyone was looking at me. Moder's new friend, Auntie Farida, asked, "Do you like your new school?"

I quickly replied, "*Tashakoor*, thank you, I like it."

In the hallway, my eyes fixed on the images of Afghanistan hanging on the walls. I stood in front of the first frame, with the full blue sky of Kabul. Scattered across the sky were the most beautiful, colourful dazzling kites. I imagined I could see my friends Hussain, Timur and Rustam flying three of them, and Rustam calling, "Hold the string tight, Timur. You will cut him off!"

From the table, Moder shouted, "Zia, don't stay up too late. You have school in the morning!"

I don't know how long I have been at my desk. My thoughts are thousands of miles away, and my notebook is still empty. What can I write about my life in Afghanistan?

• HISTORICAL NOTE •

Zia's experiences reflect an historical reality that prevailed in Afghanistan in the early 1990s. His story takes place over a decade after the former Soviet Union (present-day Russia) invaded Afghanistan to support the formation of a communist political party that seized governmental authority. The country experienced great violence and instability as US-backed armed groups resisted the government forces and the Soviet army. These armed groups, known as the Mujahideen, adopted a narrow and rigid version of Islam and eventually evolved into what became known as the Taliban.

In the period depicted at the beginning of *Zia's Story*, the Soviet Union had withdrawn from Afghanistan after having occupied the country for almost 10 years. In 1992, the Soviet-supported government of Mohammed Najibullah was ousted from power by the Mujahideen, who took control of the capital, Kabul, resulting in a civil war that cost many thousands of lives. The Taliban, emerging as the dominant power, eventually captured Kabul in 1996. They ruled with great brutality until they were ousted in 2001 by a US-led coalition of forces, which included Canada and the UK. This US-led coalition—which occupied Afghanistan for 20 years—installed a government headed at first by Hamid Karzai. Its aim was to remove the Taliban as a viable force, but it never succeeded. In 2021, the Taliban launched a major offensive as US and international forces were withdrawing from the country. In August of that year, the Taliban captured territory across Afghanistan, leading to the collapse of the US-backed government and the return of Taliban rule. This ushered in similar repressive conditions and laws to those depicted in this book—set in the 1990s—giving rise to grave concerns about the state of human rights in Afghanistan today, particularly the rights of women and girls.

· ·

The publisher wishes to thank Dr Naveena Naqvi and
Dr Allen Feldman for their editorial advice with this book.

Text copyright © 2024 by Shahnaz Qayumi
Illustrations © 2024 by Nahid Kazemi
Published in Canada, the UK and in the US in 2024.

LIBRARY AND ARCHIVES CANADA CATALOGUING IN PUBLICATION

Title: Zia's story / Shahnaz Qayumi ; illustrated by Nahid Kazemi.
Names: Qayumi, Shahnaz, author. | Kazemi, Nahid, illustrator.
Identifiers: Canadiana (print) 20240336445 | Canadiana (ebook) 20240342208 | ISBN 9781990598128
(hardcover) | ISBN 9781990598142 (softcover) | ISBN 9781990598135 (EPUB)
Subjects: LCGFT: Novels.
Classification: LCC PS8633.A98 Z23 2024 | DDC jC813/.6—dc23

Book design by Elisa Gutiérrez

The text is set in Adobe Garamond Pro. Titles are set in HVD Bodedo.

10 9 8 7 6 5 4 3 2 1

Printed and bound in Canada. The paper in this book came from
Forest Stewardship Certified and Sustainable Forestry Initiative fibers.

The publisher thanks the Government of Canada, the Canada Council for the Arts and
Livres Canada Books for their financial support. We also thank the Government of the
Province of British Columbia for the financial support we have received through the
Book Publishing Tax Credit program and the British Columbia Arts Council.

Supported by the Province of British Columbia